KNOTS Cart...
Celebrating tl
Copyright © 2010

GW01454470

KNOTS Weather Rock:

SUNNY WITH A CHANCE OF TORNADO

© 2010 RLDiesslin

for additional copies of this or other fine KNOTS merchandise, please visit the offical KNOTS website at:

www.KampKnots.com

or the main website at:
www.the-cartoonist.com

LCCN: 2010921744
First Printing April 2010
ISBN: 978-0-9702244-8-4

Published by
Diesslin Press, 1366 Town Hall Rd., Dayton, OH 45432
info@KampKnots.com
Printed in Korea.

KNOTS Cartoons
Celebrating the Fun in Scouting

The Origin of "KNOTS or Not" Scouting Cartoons

I stumbled across the US Scouting Service Project and realized that I'd struck scouting gold. What a great website! Then I noticed there was a guy named Michael Bowman who was very involved with it. I wondered if it could be the man I worked for as a scout in the trading post at Cary Camp in Indiana way back in 1971. I e-mailed him and sure enough it was. In addition to rekindling our friendship, we got to talking and came up with the idea that a monthly scouting cartoon would be a lot of fun for the USScouts.org and my own websites. The original KNOTS or Not concept was to have fun with silly situations that you would NOT do or find in scouting (sort of humorous opposites). Very quickly it evolved into a more general cartoon format ... sometimes "nots" and sometimes just silliness. Even so the name remains and is sometimes shortened to KNOTS.

Dedication

I'd like to dedicate this book to my wife, Mindy, who keeps putting up with my crazy attempt at cartooning as an occupation; my kids, Grady, Sally and Neil - scouts all; and to Michael Bowman, Cary Camp Trading Post Manager emeritus and U.S. Scouting Service Project web guru whose idea it was to start a monthly scouting cartoon!

Disclaimer

A word about the Boy Scouts of America. While they have no direct association with these cartoons, it is this great organization that has developed character, values and fraternity through fun and adventure for 100 years that inspires it. Thanks BSA and Happy 100th Birthday!

FOREWORD

Scouting is a game with a purpose. These words of Lord Robert Baden-Powell, the founder of Scouting, ring just as true today as they did decades ago. Scouting has always been an interesting experiment where learning, character development, fitness, citizenship and personal core values are the by-product of a fun game full of activities that is most often played in an outdoors setting - - camping, hiking, canoeing, climbing, and much more.

Communicating the idea of Scouting as a game is sometimes hard to do with words alone. Baden-Powell realized that frequently the best way to get a point across was with a humorous sketch and was well know for his pen and ink cartoon-like drawings. Following in that same vein, Rich Diesslin has been creating Scouting cartoons for more than a decade. His cartoons help us understand that there will be humorous moments anytime you have world-wise adults leading, coaching and counseling enthusiastic and sometimes precocious youth in a game with a purpose. Rich's cartoons are sometimes instructional, often thought-provoking and mostly just good fun with the added benefit of helping us all along in this game with a purpose.

Rich's cartoons have appeared monthly on the website of the U.S. Scouting Service Project, in the daily newspaper of the Boy Scouts of America National Jamboree, and elsewhere. Now I am delighted to see his best Scouting cartoons all in one place - in a book that begs to be opened by a campfire after a long day's hike for a bit of humor and good fun.

More than 40 years ago both Rich and I worked together on the staff of Cary Camp in Lafayette, Indiana, and though we have never met again since that wonderful summer, we've been in touch regularly - most often sharing an enduring love of the adventure of Scouting. That love of Scouting shines through in Rich's wonderful cartoons as well as his lifelong commitment to active leadership in the Scouting Movement where most recently he has served as a Camp Director.

It is with great pleasure that I recommend this wonderful collection of Scouting cartoons to the Scouting community.

Mike

Michael F. Bowman
Vice President, Web Services
U.S. Scouting Service Project
Eagle Scout 1967

DEN MEETINGS ARE FUN!

Tigers

CUB LEADERS GO THE EXTRA MILE

Cubs Under the Big Top

WHERE'S THE BIRTHDAY PARTY?

Cub Scout Blue and Gold Banquet

THAT WAS A GREAT 7-COURSE DINNER, FOLLOWED BY TWO HOURS OF AWARDS. NOW, AFTER WE AWARD THE AWARD FOR AWARDING THE MOST AWARDS, WE WILL HAVE A MINUTE-BY-MINUTE ACCOUNT OF A THREE-WEEK CIVIL WAR BATTLE...

© 2003 RLDiesslin

CUBMASTER WARDROBE MALFUNCTION

BEAR Rank

CONGRATS ON EARNING THE RANK OF BEAR!

HUH?!

RLDiesslin © 2008

CUBS

THE CUB SCOUT TROPHY ROOM!

Cub Scout Vest

9/02 © 2002 R.L.Diesslin

IF YOU DON'T RUN THE MEETING, THEY WILL!

Den Meetings

YES, MADGE I'M TELLING YOU IT WAS AMAZING ...

4/03 © 2002 R.L.Diesslin

SCOUTS KNOW WHAT'S FUN!

Cub Scout Equipment

I WANT A POCKET KNIFE, FLASHLIGHT, SLEEPING BAG, TENT, SOME COOKWARE ...

DON'T YA JUST LOVE IT!?

12/09 RLDiesslin © 2009

KEEP IT AGE APPROPRIATE!

Den Field Trips

COUNTY JAIL

DO YOU WANT THE SCARED STRAIGHT TOUR ...

AH, NO. THIS IS A FIELD TRIP NOT REHAB!

YEAH! SCARED STRAIGHT! YES!

COOL!

<GULP> HELP!

© 2002 RLDiesslin
8/02

HELP YOUR CUB SCOUT DO <u>HIS</u> BEST
Pinewood Derby

CUB SCOUTS - FUN FOR ALL AGES!
Pinewood Derby

FUN FOR THE WHOLE FAMILY!

EXPLORING THE GREAT OUTDOORS

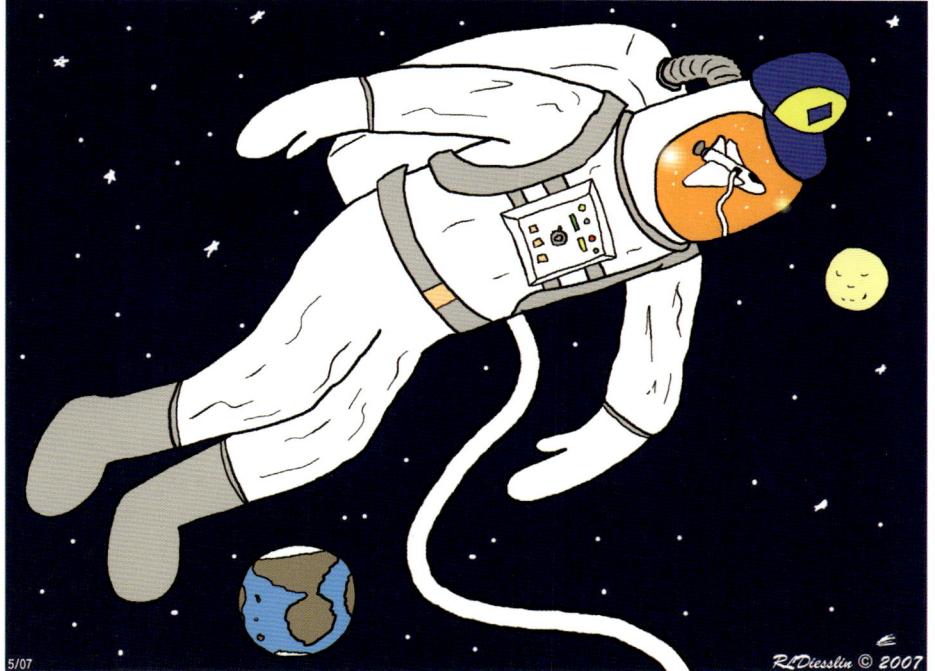

KEEP THE TASK DOABLE!

WEBELOS Handyman Activity Pin

SSSSSH! BE VERY, VERY QUIET ...

WEBELOS Troop Visitation

MAKING THE JUMP TO BOY SCOUTS

ONLY CUT IN THE DESIGNATED AREA

JUST HANGING AROUND

Communing with Nature

BIKE HIKE MYSTERY REVEALED

Bike Hike

PLAN AHEAD
Camp Gadgets

WHEN EXTREME CAMP GADGETING ...

UM, A LITTLE HELP PLEASE!

10/09 RLDiesslin © 2009

REMEMBER TO LASH FROM THE OUTSIDE!

MMMM - LET'S EAT!
Camp Food

RLDiesslin © 2009

LUNCH

KAMP KOOKIN'

Kamp Knots:

or you could be eating ...

Seabase Today:

Burgers
Fries
Pears
Milk
Cookies

EEW! THAT'S DISGUSTING!

Squid
Barnacles
Seaweed
Saltwater
Mud

YEAH! WHY DON'T WE GET COOL FOOD LIKE THAT!

8/09

SUMMERCAMP: HOME AWAY FROM HOME!

Campfires

Overheard at the week's final campfire ...

AT FIRST I WAS HOMESICK ... NOW I'LL PROBABLY BE CAMPSICK FOR AWHILE!

YEAH! ME TOO.

© 2003 RLDiesslin

SUMMER CAMP TRADITIONS: COUNSELOR TOTEMS

Camp Dining

The scouts quickly learned NOT to grab Paul Bunyan's totem if they wanted to get enough to eat...

© 2003 RLDiesslin

YOU NEVER KNOW WHAT YOU'LL FIND!

Caving Anyone?

ALL WRAPPED UP IN SCOUTING

Climbing

EVEN COOKING CAN BE AN ADVENTURE

Cooking

THANK YOU FOR A CENTURY OF FUN & VALUES!

Boy Scouts of America

KNOCK YOUR FIRE OUT COLD

ALWAYS BE SAFE WITH FIRE

WHAT NOT TO DO IN A THUNDERSTORM! Safety

PITCH YOUR TENT ON HIGH GROUND! Location

PLAN S.M.A.R.T.

National Jamboree Gateways

WOW! THAT WILL BE SOME GATEWAY!

TOO BAD JAMBO ENDED YESTERDAY.

© 2001 RLDiesslin

Jamboree Today Newspaper 7/31/01

KNOW HOW TO USE YOUR EQUIPMENT

GPS Navigation

I THINK THIS SAYS WE'RE GETTING CLOSE!

REALLY? BECAUSE THIS DOESN'T LOOK LIKE KANSAS ANYMORE.

KAMP KNOTS

KAMP KNOTS

RLDiesslin © 2009

BE PREPARED FOR THE WEATHER!

KNOW YOUR ~~TOYS~~ EQUIPMENT

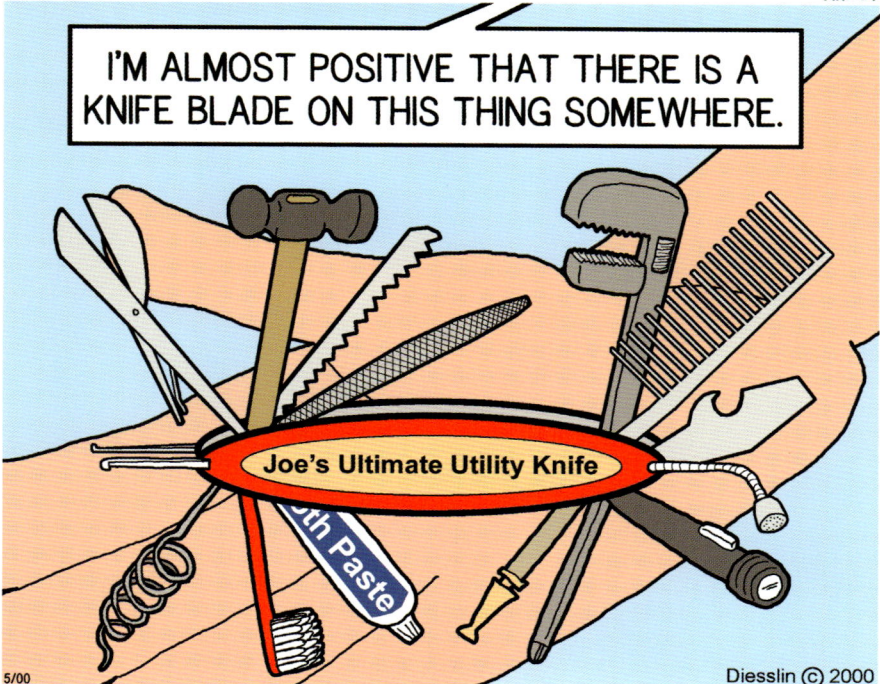

KNOW YOUR KNOTS ... REALLY!

Knot Tieing

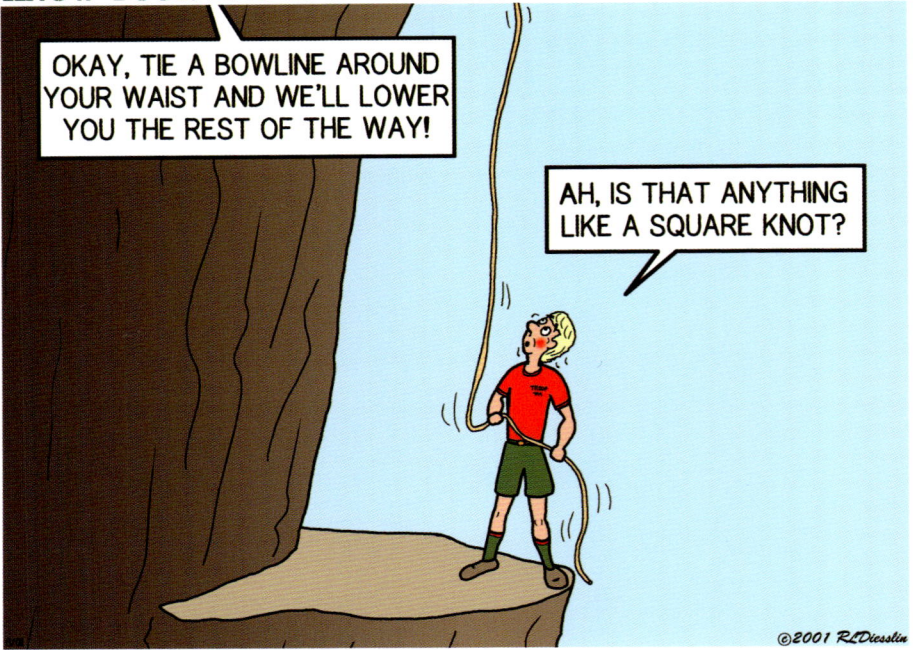

OKAY, TIE A BOWLINE AROUND YOUR WAIST AND WE'LL LOWER YOU THE REST OF THE WAY!

AH, IS THAT ANYTHING LIKE A SQUARE KNOT?

©2001 RLDiesslin

PLAN A PRACTICAL LOCATION FOR ALL FACILITIES

Location

WOW! JOE REALLY DID A NICE JOB ON THE LATRINE.

YEAH, JUST A BIT FAR ... I CAN BARELY MAKE OUT THE CAMP DOWN THERE IN THE VALLEY ...

LATRINE
CAMP

11/00 © 2000 Rich Diesslin

THERE'S NO SUCH THING AS OVER-TRAINED

Scouter Training

HEY! I WAS TRAINED IN 1948 AND IT WAS GOOD ENOUGH FOR THEN, SO IT'S GOOD ENOUGH FOR NOW ... WHIPPER-SNAPPER!

THE CODGER DOTH PROTEST TOO MUCH, METHINKS.

5/09 RLDiesslin © 2008

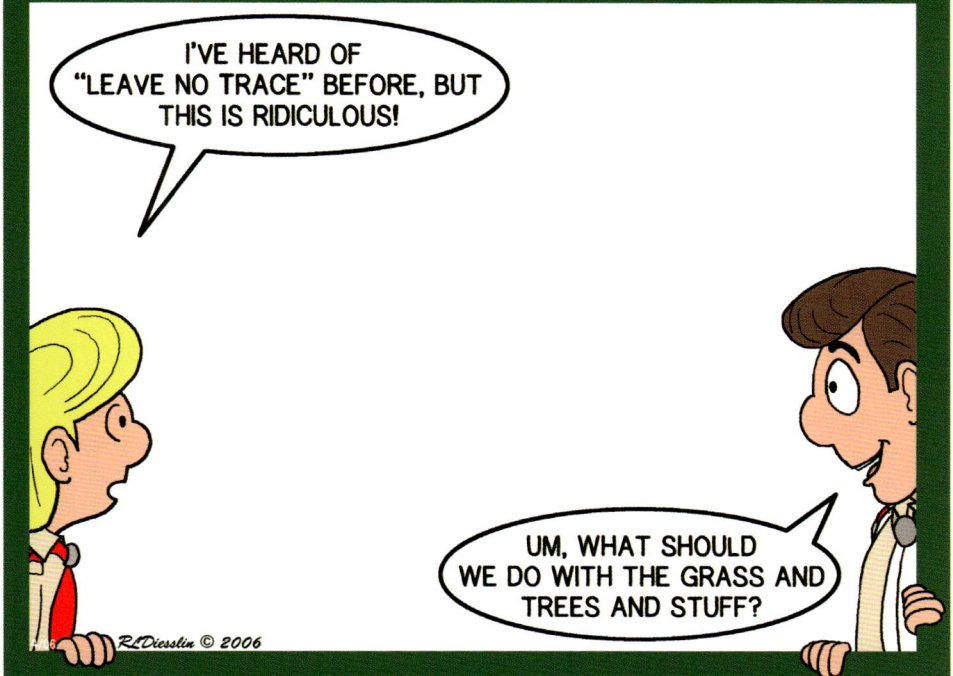

OKAY, LEAVE THE GOOD STUFF!

Leave No Trace

I'VE HEARD OF "LEAVE NO TRACE" BEFORE, BUT THIS IS RIDICULOUS!

UM, WHAT SHOULD WE DO WITH THE GRASS AND TREES AND STUFF?

RLDiesslin © 2006

ALWAYS LEAVE IT BETTER THAN YOU FOUND IT! Leave No Trace

GOOD EATS - BETTER FEATS

Meal Planning

A SCOUT IS CHEERFUL!

Mile Swim

SORRY. THERE IS NO PATCH FOR THE **SMILE** SWIM!

6/06

MFBIRLD © 2006

BE PREPARED ... BUT LET'S NOT BE SILLY!

Cooking

YOU KNOW, THERE IS SUCH A THING AS BEING OVER-PREPARED.

MAYBE, BUT THIS IS A COOKING CAMPOREE. OH, THERE'S THE BELL, TIME TO CHECK THE POT ROAST!

Ding! Ding!

3/00

© 2000 RLDiesslin

100% CHANCE OF WEATHER

Underwater Camping Award

QUESTION: DOES IT RAIN AT CAMP?
ANSWER:

IS THIS INTRO TO SCUBA?

NOPE. THIS IS OUR CAMPSITE!

© 2001 R.Dissler

modified Jamboree Today Newspaper 7/30/01

RANGER CORPS - KEEPING THE CAMP RUNNING!

Ranger Appreciation

PSST - HEY RANGER, THE COAST IS CLEAR, YOU CAN COME DOWN NOW!

NO, NO - IT'S PEACEFUL UP HERE. BESIDES YOU'RE JUST TRYING TO TRICK ME INTO FIXING SOMETHING YOU CAN FIX!

THAT'S NOT TRUE. WE JUST REALLY LIKE TALKING WITH YOU. OH AND THE COFFEE POT IS RUNNING SLOW AND ...

6/09

R.Dissler © 2008

SCOUTS SHOULD BE SELF-PROPELLED

Scout-Run

I SAID I'D LET THE SCOUTS RUN IT ON THEIR OWN, BUT IT'S DARN NEAR KILLING ME! DON'T JUST STAND THERE, HELP DUCT TAPE ME TO THIS CHAIR.

SERVICE WITH A SMILE!

Service Projects

ADOPT-A-HIGHWAY MEANS KEEP IT CLEAN. YOU CAN'T RUN A TOLL BOOTH!

TOLL

ADOPT-A-HIGHWAY PROGRAM

USE A GOOD CHECKLIST

Bugs

A GOOD NIGHT'S SLEEP MAKES THE DAY GO BETTER!

Sleep Deprivation

IT'S KNOTS SOUP

PLAY IT COOL

FOLLOW BSA SAFE SWIM DEFENSE

Safety

9/99
©1999 RLDiesslin

RADICAL RESTROOM ROLE REVERSAL

Scouters

One of the benefits for women scout leaders ...

7/02 LWist
© 2002 RLDiesslin

CRITTERS TO WATCH FOR IN THE WOOODS

11/07

A STICK SHY OF A BUNDLE?

WELL I'M READY FOR JOEL'S BOARD OF REVIEW, BUT THIS SEEMS LIKE AN ODD SYSTEM.

FRANK, YOU'RE KILLING ME HERE!

REVIEW

1/10

RLGiesslin © 2010

ADVANCING ALONG THE SCOUTING TRAIL

Tenderfoot Rank

TRAVELING IN STYLE

First Class Scout

THE JUDGES AGREE - STAR SCOUT ROCKS!

Scouting Idol

STAR RANK IS JUST WHO YOU ARE. YOU REALLY LOOK GOOD IN IT!

WELL, I REALLY HATE TO SAY IT, BUT THAT WAS SPECTACULAR. KEEP THAT UP AND WE'LL SEE YOU HERE AGAIN!

YO, YO, DAWG! CHECK IT OUT! STAR SCOUT IS DA BOMB!

2/08

RLDiesslin © 2007

SCOUTING IS NO WITCH HUNT

If the Tin Man had been a Boy Scout ...

IT IS MY GREAT HONOR TO AWARD YOU THIS HEART FOR EARNING RANK OF LIFE SCOUT!

11/08

RLDiesslin © 2008

ENJOY THE VIEW!

Eagle Scout

IT'S NOT THE HIGHEST RANK IN BOY SCOUTS FOR NOTHING!

© 2001 RLDiesslin

SCOUTING IS FOR THE BIRDS!

Eagle Scout

SON, WE ARE ALL PROUD OF YOUR EAGLE RANK BUT YOU HAVE TO GIVE UP THE NEST ...

I'LL TAKE IT!

2/05

RLDiesslin © 2004

SCOUT EAGLES

SOMEDAY I WANT TO BE A SCOUT!

YOU NEVER KNOW WHO YOU MIGHT MEET!

HOW THE LONE RANGER AND TONTO REALLY MET ...

YOU'RE ORDER OF THE ARROW TOO!?! COOL.

2/00

©2000 RLDiesslin

KNOTS

GOT DANCE!?!

ORDER OF THE ARROW

I DON'T THINK THIS IS WHAT IS MEANT ...
BUT IT TAKES ANIMAL SCIENCE TO A NEW LEVEL!

3/03

© 2002 RLDiesslin

ROBIN HOOD GOES TO SCOUT CAMP ...

Archery Merit Badge

AH, ROBIN, WE'RE VERY
IMPRESSED WITH YOUR SHOOING, HOWEVER,
WE'RE GOING TO HAVE TO START CHARGING
YOU FOR ARROWS!

9/00

© 2000 RLDiesslin

WHO KNOWS WHERE YOUR ART MIGHT LEAD?

Art Merit Badge

COUNSELORS REVIEW YOUNG CLAUDE MONET'S ART PROJECT ...

WELL, IT'S JUST A BUNCH OF COLORED DOTS, BUT IT'S KINDA NICE ... LET'S COUNT IT.

© 2001 RLDiesslin

9/01

LOOP HOLES IN SCOUTING ARE FOR YOUR BELT

Astronomy Merit Badge

SORRY, BUT I DON'T SEE ANYWAY TO COUNT A SKETCH OF YOUR DOG "MOON ROVER" FOR REQUIREMENT 7.

GRRRR

craters

RLDiesslin © 2007

1/08

HE AIN'T HEAVY, HE'S MY BROTHER

Backpacking Merit Badge

I THOUGHT THIS WAS A LITTLE HEAVIER THAN USUAL!

I'M GLAD YOU'RE LAUGHING BECAUSE GUESS WHERE THE GEAR IS?

10/07

RLDiesslin © 2007

EXTREME BACKPACKING?!

Backpacking Merit Badge

WOW, A JET PACK! IT'S AWESOME, BUT HOW MUCH GEAR CAN IT HOLD?

WELL, I'VE GOT MY LUNCH ALONG!

© 2002 RLDiesslin

MAKE IT INTERESTING - CHALLENGE YOURSELF!

Basketry Merit Badge

LET ME GUESS. YOU WANTED A CHALLENGE, BUT THE SNORKELING GEAR WASN'T AVAILABLE!?

© 2002 RLDiesslin

WATCH THE BIRDIE

Bird Study Merit Badge

9/05 RLDiesslin © 2005

BE PREPARED TO ACHIEVE

THERE'S A FEW THINGS MISSING.
THE SCOUTMASTER'S SIGNATURE,
THE MERIT BADGE NAME,
THE REQUIREMENT NUMBERS.
IS THIS YOUR FIRST BADGE?

OK. WHAT'S NEEDED?
OK,
OK,
OK.
OH NO. I'M A LIFE SCOUT!

9/09

RLDiesslin © 2009

BUGLING IS NOT A SMALL BUG

OKAY, REVEILLE ON 3 GUYS!
REALLY LOUD. THE SCOUTMASTER
DID SAY "SURPRISE ME!"

5/08

RLDiesslin © 2007

CAMPING WITH THE   **BEST**   Camping Merit Badge

WHERE'D THE BOONE KID LEARN THAT?

I HEARD IT ALL STARTED WITH CAMPING MERIT BADGE.

11/05   RLDiesslin © 2005

KEEP THE OBJECTIVE IN MIND   Canoeing Merit Badge

THE IDEA OF SWAMPING THE CANOE IS TO PRACTICE UN-SWAMPING IT ...

OH, NOW YOU TELL ME!

8/03   © 2002 RLDiesslin

THE ELEMENT OF FUN!

I THINK I'VE DISCOVERED A NEW ELEMENT ... SCOUTONIUM!

11/03 © 2002 RLDiesslin

COUNSELORS LIKE ENTHUSIASM

BILLY IMPRESSES HIS CINEMATOGRAPHY COUNSELOR ...

AH ... I REALLY LIKE THE REALISM ... NOW HAVE IT PUT ME DOWN!

DIRECTOR

10/01 © 2001 RLDiesslin

THE JOURNEY OF 1,000" BEGINS 1" AT A TIME!

Climbing Merit Badge

I ... I ... DON'T THINK I'M GOING TO MAKE IT, PAL! JUST GO ON WITHOUT ME!

DUDE! WE HAVEN'T EVEN STARTED CLIMBING YET!

3/08

RLDiesslin © 2007

MERIT BADGE OR HOBBY? YES!

Coin Collecting Merit Badge

I THINK THE IDEA BEHIND COIN COLLECTING IS TO GET ONE OF EACH KIND, NOT ALL OF THE SAME KIND ...

OH, WELL, I GUESS THAT WOULD BE EASIER NOW, WOULDN'T IT!?!

12/03

© 2002 RLDiesslin

SCOUTING - IT'S CONTAGIOUS

OH LOOK, IT'S THE SCOUTING VIRUS! IT DOESN'T AFFECT YOUR PC, IT JUST MAKES YOU WANT TO GO CAMPING!

EVEN THE ANTI-VIRUS SOFTWARE IS PITCHING A TENT!

9/03

© 2002 RLDiesslin

FAMOUS SCOUTING RECIPES

FROM THE "IT COULD HAPPEN" FILE:

THEN BAM! THERE YOU HAVE IT ... A FOIL DINNER!

Gourmet

11/01

© 2001 RLDiesslin

PREVENT MORE THAN JUST FOREST FIRES!   Crime Prevention Merit Badge

STICK TO BRUSHING YOUR TEETH!   Dentistry Merit Badge

TRAINING GONE WRONG?

CARING IS THE KEY

BADGES

CREATIVITY COMES IN MANY FORMS!

Electricity Merit Badge

SKIP FRANKENSTEIN DID GO ON TO FINISH HIS ELECTRICITY MERIT BADGE ...

I DON'T THINK THERE'S A REQUIREMENT TO REGENERATE LIFE WITH ELECTRICITY, BUT MAYBE WE CAN FIND SOME WAY TO USE IT!

1/02

© 2001 RLDiesslin

BE PREPARED

Engineering Merit Badge

YOU MEAN THE ONLY THING KEEPING THE CONTAINMENT SHIELD CLOSED IS A SQUARE KNOT?

YEP. JUST OUR GOOD FORTUNE A BOY SCOUT TROOP WAS TOURING THE PLANT TODAY!

REACTOR CORE

DANGER

DANGER

12/05 RLDiesslin © 200

ALL THE CLUES POINT TOWARD SCOUTING!

HOOKED ON SCOUTING

LEARN FROM THE EXPERTS!

Forestry Merit Badge

AND HERE'S OUR KAMP KNOTS FORESTRY MERIT BADGE COUNSELOR ...

WHOA!

10/04

© 2003 RxDiesslin

DO YOU HAVE A GREEN THUMB?

Gardening Merit Badge

NICE REPLICA OF THE GARDEN OF EDEN JOEY!

AH, THAT APPLE'S NOT FROM THE TREE I SAID NOT TO TOUCH IS IT?

4/05

RxDiesslin ©2005

DISCOVER YOUR ROOTS IN SCOUTING!

Genealogy Merit Badge

"ROUGH"ING IT IN SCOUTS

Golf Merit Badge

BUILD CHARACTER, REPAIR BUILDINGS

Home Repair Merit Badge

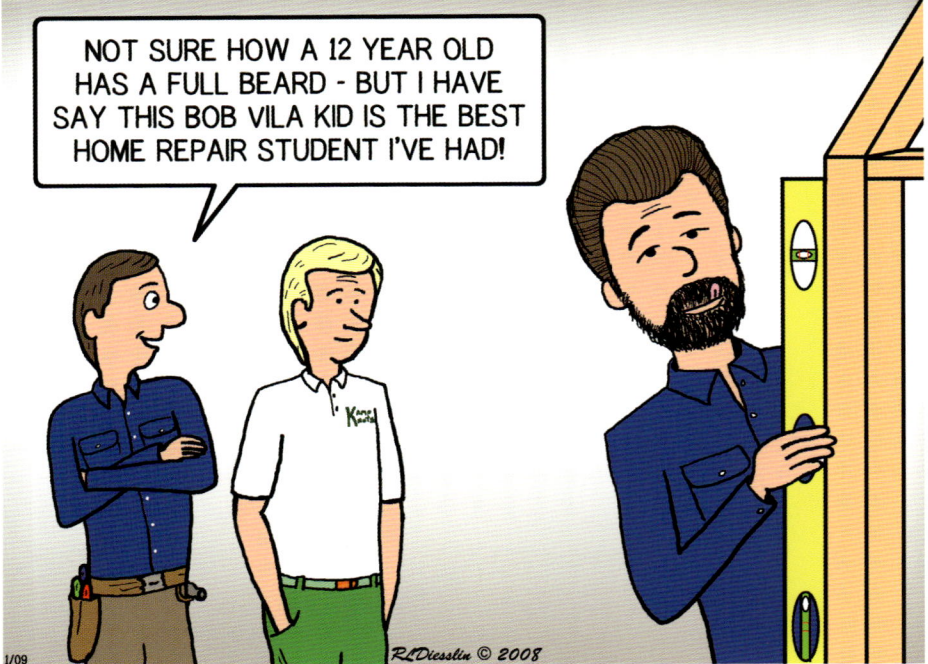

NOT SURE HOW A 12 YEAR OLD HAS A FULL BEARD - BUT I HAVE SAY THIS BOB VILA KID IS THE BEST HOME REPAIR STUDENT I'VE HAD!

1/09

RLDiesslin © 2008

READ THE MANUAL!

Horsemanship Merit Badge

INTERESTING, BUT NO. THAT'S NOT THE HORSEMANSHIP WE'RE LOOKING FOR!

RLDiesslin © 2006

INQUIRING MINDS WANT TO KNOW

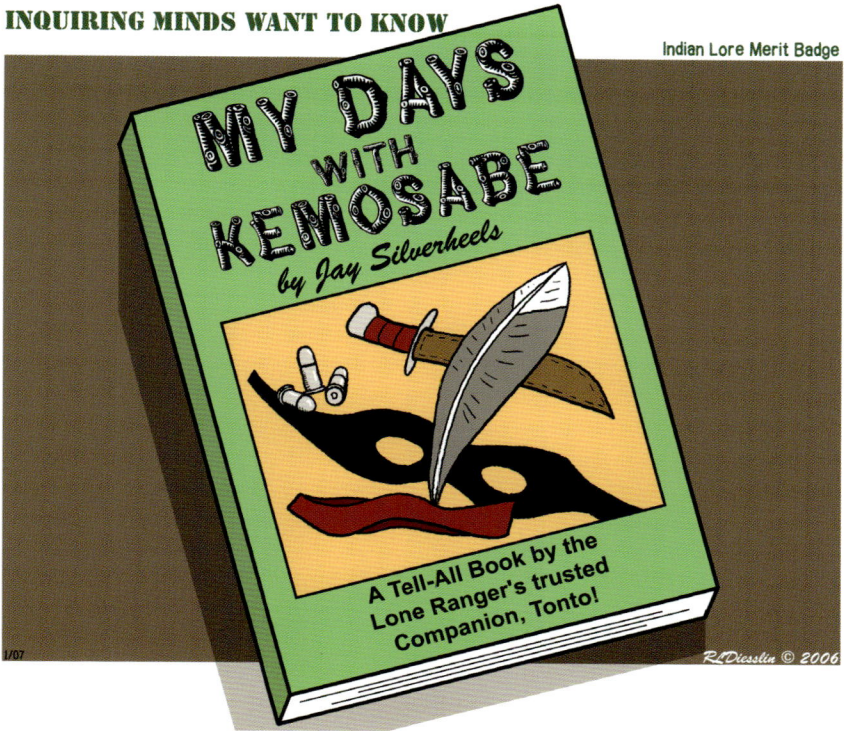

MY DAYS WITH KEMOSABE
by Jay Silverheels

A Tell-All Book by the Lone Ranger's trusted Companion, Tonto!

1/07

RLDiesslin © 2006

THE SCIENCE OF FUN!

I COULD WATCH THESE GUYS FOR HOURS.

YEAH, AND THEY SEEM SO ORGANIZED.

ACME SCOUT FARM

10/05

RLDiesslin © 2005

AQUA-BOY TAKES LIFESAVING

Lifesaving Merit Badge

YES, A RESCUE WITH A TEAM OF SEA CREATURES COULD COUNT AS "GOING WITH ASSISTANCE" - WE JUST CAN'T TEACH IT THAT WAY.

3/06

RLDiesslin © 2005

SCOUTING - IT'S INVINCIBLE!

Metal Working Merit Badge

SURE, IF YOU CAN CREATE A REAL OPERATIONAL IRON MAN ARMOR I'D COUNT THAT FOR METAL WORKING.

IF!?

6/08

RLDiesslin © 2008

SCOUTING: LARGER THAN LIFE

Model Design and Building Merit Badge

I'LL COUNT IT BUT I THINK YOU NEED TO REVIEW THE PART ABOUT SCALING.

WHAT? 12 TO 1 MEANS 12 TIMES LARGER THAN ACTUAL RIGHT!?!

10/08

RLDiesslin © 2008

A RELATIVE PERHAPS?

Nuclear Science Merit Badge

ATOMIC ENERGY TENT

THERE'S SOMETHING VERY FAMILIAR ABOUT OUR ENERGY MERIT BADGE COUNSELOR ...

© 2009 RLDiesslin
Jamboree Today
Newpaper 7/28/01

SCUBA ... THE REST OF THE STORY

Oceanography Merit Badge

1943: YOUNG JACQUES COUSTEAU EARNS HIS OCEANOGRAPHY MERIT BADGE ...

YOU CAN BREATH UNDER ZE WATER ... I CALL IT ZE AQUALUNG

NIFTY! I THINK YOU SHOULD RENAME IT WITH AN OBSCURE ACRONYM THOUGH ...

2/02

© 2002 RLDiesslin

SCOUTS ARE ATTRACTED TO FUN

Orienteering Merit Badge

ODD, OUR COMPASS ROUTE KEEPS RETURNING TO THE ICE CREAM STAND!

I SEE NO REASON TO ARGUE WITH THE MAP! YOUR TURN TO BUY!

MAGNETIC NORTH ICE CREAM & TREATS

8/06 RLDiesslin © 2006

GET THE PICTURE?

YOUNG ANSEL ADAMS WORKS ON HIS PHOTOGRAPHY MERIT BADGE ...

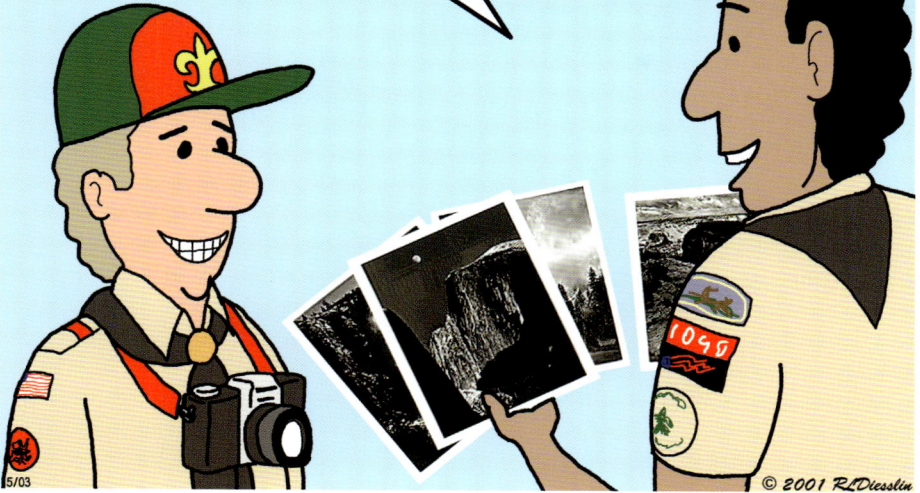

HEY! THESE ARE GREAT! HAVE YOU EVER CONSIDERED USING COLOR FILM?

5/03

© 2001 RLDiesslin

THERE'S STILL PIONEERING TO DO!

NO QUESTION SIR, IT'S THE REMAINS OF A MONKEY BRIDGE!

ON MARS! BUT HOW ...

OOPS! GOTTA GO ...

3/04

© 2003 RLDiesslin

YOU NEVER KNOW WHAT YOU'LL DISCOVER

Plant Science Merit Badge

THIS IS NOT WHAT I WAS EXPECTING!

I DON'T EVEN WANT TO KNOW WHAT'S IN THERE!

Seymour? Seymour? Where are you?!

4/04

RLDiesslin © 2003

KNOW THE REQUIREMENTS

Plumbing Merit Badge

NO. I CAN'T COUNT THE 3-D PIPE SCREEN-SAVER TOWARD YOUR PLUMBING MERIT BADGE ...

4/02

© 2001 RLDiesslin

THERE IS DRAMA IN NATURE!

Reptile & Amphibian Study Merit Badge

DON'T MOVE! THAT'S AN EXOTIC BREED. JUST LOOK AT THE FANGS ON THAT ONE!

IT'S A TADPOLE IN A JAR. THERE ARE NO FANGS. JUST TAKE THE PICTURE ALREADY!

8/04

RLDiesslin © 2004

NEVER SQUIRT A GIFT HORSE IN THE MOUTH

Rifle Shooting Merit Badge

NO, THE SUPER-SQUIRTER 2000 DOES NOT COUNT TOWARD YOUR RIFLE SHOOTING MERIT BADGE.

WELL, OKAY I THINK I'LL GO ASK THE OTHER COUNSELORS JUST IN CASE!

8/08

RLDiesslin © 2008

BE NICE TO YOUR COUNSELORS!

Rowing Merit Badge

SATISFACTION: A JOB WELL DONE!

Salesmanship Merit Badge

THINK BIG!

I THOUGHT YOU WERE GOING TO DO A SCALE MODEL OUT OF CLAY!

I GUESS I JUST GOT CARRIED-AWAY!

5/03

© 2002 RLDiesslin

SPONSORING SCOUTING ALWAYS PAYS OFF!

Shotgun Shooting Merit Badge

PULL!

SPONSORING THE SHOTGUN SHOOTING MERIT BADGE HAS REALLY LOWERED MY PRODUCTION COST!

Knots Kamp

SWISS SKEET

Mr. Molds, CEO
Swiss Cheese Co.

3/05 RLDiesslin © 2005

FUN AT CAMP!

(Really) Small Boat Sailing Merit Badge

YOU MIGHT BE ABLE TO USE THAT FOR MODEL BUILDING, BUT THAT'S NOT WHAT IS MEANT BY SMALL BOAT SAILING!

KAMP KNOTS

KAMP KNOTS

6/03

© 2002 RLDiesslin

SCOUTING OUT HIGH ADVENTURE

Snow Sports Merit Badge

I'M SNOW-BORED!

ME TOO. LET'S GO EXCHANGE FOR SKIS!

3/05

RLDiesslin © 2005

THE EAGLE SCOUT HAS LANDED

Space Exploration Merit Badge

I'M SORRY MR. ARMSTRONG, BUT THE SPACE EXPLORATION MERIT BADGE IS FOR SCOUTS UNDER THE AGE OF 18.

DANG!

Jamboree Today
Newspaper 7/27/01
© 2001 RLDiesslin

COUNSELORS HAVE FUN TOO!

Surveying Merit Badge

ARE YOU YOUNG FELLERS SURVEYORS? CAUSE I NEED TO STAKE A CLAIM!

VERY FUNNY MR. BOWMAN. NOW COULD YOU SHOW US HOW TO USE THIS THING!

RLDiesslin © 2008

BADGES

SCOUTS ENJOY THE RIDE!

Swimming Merit Badge

NOW THAT'S CLOTHES INFLATION!

♪ I float! I float! ♪ ...

WHO KNEW WEIRD AL WOULD BE HERE?

6/05 RLDiesslin © 2005

WATCH FOR REQUIREMENT CHANGES!

Weather Merit Badge

KNOWING ALL THE WEATHER ROCK LORE DOESN'T REALLY COUNT TOWARD THE WEATHER MERIT BADGE!

ODD, IT SEEMS MORE ACCURATE THAN MODERN METHODS!

6/0 2002 © RLDiesslin

ROUGHING IT FOR THE FUN OF IT!

Wilderness Survival Merit Badge

SAM!?!

HOWDY! I'M WORKING ON MY WILDERNESS SURVIVAL. WANT SOME SASSAFRAS TEA!?!

10/03

© 2002 RLDiesslin

BOTTOMLINE: SCOUTING IS FUN!

Fish and Wildlife Management Merit Badge

REPORTING FOR WORK BOSS!

The Buck Stops Out There

WILDLIFE

PRODUCTION

WIDGETS CO.

WALLEYE STREET JOURNAL

PRESIDENT

WELL OKAY, BUT IT IS SATURDAY YOU KNOW!

10/06

RLDiesslin © 2006

CARVE OUT YOUR NICHE IN SCOUTING!

Wood Carving Merit Badge

MAKING SCOUT HISTORY

Woodworking Merit Badge

LEARNING TO C.O.P.E.

BSA's Challenging Outdoor Personal Experience

Survivor's Probst at COPE training ...

JEFF, TRUST ME ON THIS ONE. IN COPE, WE DON'T VOTE PEOPLE OFF AFTER THE CHALLENGE!

I GET IT, BUT I JUST DON'T GET IT!

3/09

RLDiesslin © 2008

NSJ: SOMETHING FOR EVERYONE!

National Scout Jamboree

THE APPLICATION SAID YOU NEEDED A BASS ...

WAS THAT UNDER BAND OR FISHING?

REGISTER for the NATIONAL JAMBOREE

WE'LL HAVE ONE REALLY HIP REVEILLE!

4/00

© 2000 RLDiesslin

FLY FISHING

Northern Tier Fly Adventure

SCOUTING - REAL ADVENTURE

Philmont

Sailing

FUN IN THE SUN

Seabase High Adventure

THIS WEEK'S HANDS-DOWN WINNER OF THE SEABASE TALENT SHOW!

NEWSFLASH: GIRLS ALLOWED!

Venture Crew

PSST, JOE! THERE'S A GIRL AT OUR MEETING.

WELL, DUH! WE'RE A VENTURE CREW.

8/10 · RLDiesslin © 2010

NOT GRASPING THE GRAVITY OF THE SITUATION

Venturing

SO IS THIS WHAT THEY MEAN BY "HIGH ADVENTURE"

NO! THIS IS WHAT THEY MEAN BY "KNOW YOUR ROUTE!"

7/08 · RLDiesslin © 2008

A SCOUT IS TRUSTWORTH

EXCUSE ME SIR, BUT YOU DROPPED YOUR WALLET BACK THERE.

GOSH, MONEY AND ALL, THANKS! SAY, THAT UNIFORM, ARE YOU THE LONE RANGER'S PAL?

HONESTY: WITHOUT IT SOCIETY FALLS APART. CHARACTER COUNTS!

© 2000 RLDiesslin

A SCOUT IS LOYAL

DUTY TO GOD COUNTRY, OTHERS AND SELF, THAT'S THE SCOUT WAY!

Diesslin © 2000

A SCOUT IS HELPFUL

YOU BOYS ARE REALLY SERIOUS ABOUT THIS HELPFUL THING, AREN'T YOU?

TAKING IT TO A NEW LEVEL!

© 2000 RLDiesslin

A SCOUT IS FRIENDLY

Scout Law

HOWDY THERE FELLA! SAY, ARE YOU NEW AROUND THESE PARTS?

HUH!?!

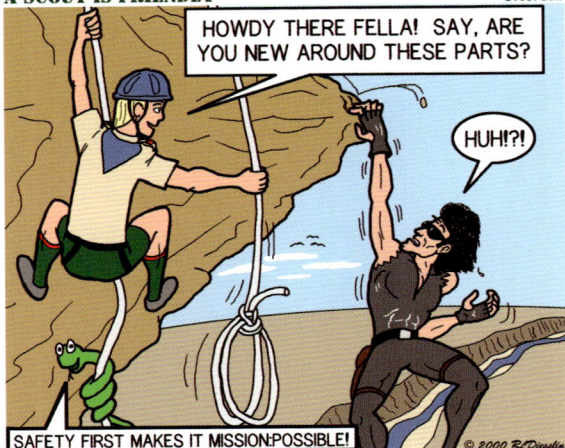

SAFETY FIRST MAKES IT MISSION:POSSIBLE!

© 2000 RLDiesslin

A SCOUT IS COURTEOUS

Scout Law

EXCUSE ME SIR, BUT YOU LOOK A LITTLE LOST. PERHAPS I CAN BE OF SOME ASSISTANCE.

GOOD MANNERS ARE ALWAYS APPROPRIATE ... YIKE!

© 2000 RLDiesslin

A SCOUT IS KIND

Scout Law
© 2000 RLDiesslin

HE'S THE BEST DEN CHIEF I'VE EVER SEEN.

OKAY, THAT'S GOOD. NOW TIE A SQUARE KNOT ...

A SCOUT IS OBEDIENT — Scout Law

YOU SAID ... "BUILD A BIG ONE."

GOOD THING HE DIDN'T SAY "OVER HOT LAVA!"

© 2000 Rich Diesslin

A SCOUT IS CHEERFUL — Scout Law

I'M A LITTLE CONCERNED ABOUT THAT BOY, HE'S ALWAYS CHEERFUL NO MATTER WHAT HE'S DOING.

YA, YA, IT ZOUNDS LIKE ACUTE BOY ZCOUT ZYNDROME!

IS THAT HEALTHY?

VERY!

© 2001 RLDiesslin

A SCOUT IS THRIFTY — Scout Law

WELL SON, YOUR MOM AND I NEED ANOTHER LOAN FROM YOUR LAWN MOWING BUSINESS ...

I DON'T KNOW DAD, YOU'RE STILL CARRYING CREDIT CARD DEBT, A MORTGAGE, A CAR LOAN AND YOU JUST DON'T SEEM TO BE ABLE TO STICK TO A BUDGET ...

REMEMBER, THE MORE YOU SAVE, THE MORE YOU HAVE!

© 2001 RLDiesslin

A SCOUT IS BRAVE

Scout Law

A SCOUT IS CLEAN

Scout Law

A SCOUT IS REVERENT

Scout Law

THINK BIG!

Scouting for the Future

I WONDER
WHAT'S
COOKING FOR
THE NEXT
100 YEARS?!

I DON'T KNOW
BUT LOOKS LIKE IT'S
GOING TO BE BIG!

I THINK THEY
ASKED THE BUNYAN
KID TO COOK!

GOOD
THING THEY
DIDN'T ASK
HIM TO DO
THE FIRE!

SCOUTING

RLDressler © 2010

7/10

ABOUT THE CARTOONIST

It all started a long time ago, after I was born ... blah, blah, blah ... zzzzz ... Hey! Wake up! Which brings me to the present where I'm a full-time, freelance cartoonist doing what cartoonists do - mixing humor, topics of interest and silly drawings to create cartoons.

I was a Cub Scout back when there were Lions instead of Tigers and Boy Scouts wore green shirts. That's the uniform I still wear on occasion much to the puzzlement of modern scouters. Honestly it's just part of being thrifty and having a mom that saved all my scout stuff. It still fits only because it was way too big when we bought it (the only one in stock at JC Penny's, our scout store back then, right before starting as summer camp staff in 1971)!

I have three scouts in my family now: two sons and a daughter. The more I am involved in scouts, the more I am convinced that it is a very important resource for developing character and values. When others talk negatively about youth today, all I can say is that they should work with scouts - then they would see the positive!

My main focus is on Christian cartooning in the form of church, biblical and theological cartoons, visual parables and commentary. However, I also keep busy on freelance projects for various magazines, journals, websites and newspapers. My Out-to-Lunch (OTL) general cartoons can be found online and in the Springfield (Ohio) Newspaper, and last but not least, I do the KNOTS or Not scouting cartoons for the U.S. Scouting Service Project and my websites.

I hope you enjoy this book as much as I enjoy cartooning and scouting! Feel free to e-mail me and/or visit my website at www.the-cartoonist.com!

Yours In Scouting,
Rich

Rich Diesslin
Cartoonist
Eagle Scout '72

Other Books by the Cartoonist

Books in Print:

KNOTS Cartoons, Celebrating the Fun in Scouting, (yes - this one!)
ISBN: 978-0-9702244-8-4 Dayton:Diesslin Press, April 2010, 80p, full color.
$12.95

A Journey Through Christian Theology, Minneapolis:Fortress Press, ISBN:
978-0-8006969-7-9, March 2010, 2nd Edition. Editor/Author William P.
Anderson. $39

The Cartoon Gospel of John, A Serious Commentary with Visual Parables,
ISBN 0-87946-273-6, Chicago:ACTA, September, 2004, p 128. Commentary
written by William P. Anderson. $12.95

The Cartoon Gospel (of Luke), ISBN 0-940169-09-6, New Berlin:Liturgical
Publications, Inc., December, 1990. $11

E-Books and Cartoon Books and Collections on CD:

KNOTS or Not Scouting Cartoon Collection, (these cartoons on CD for
newsletters, etc.), ISBN: 978-0-9702244-6-0, and annual supplements. $19.00

Joseph: A Tale of Two Traditions, ISBN 0-9702244-7-8, February, 2007.
$15

The Cartoon Ten Commandments, ISBN 0-9702244-2-7, October, 2000.
$15

The Cartoon Gospels, ISBN 0-9702244-5-1, September, 2002. $20

The Cartoon Gospel of Mark, ISBN 0-9702244-4-3, September, 2002. $15

The Cartoon Gospel of Matthew, ISBN 0-9702244-3-5, October, 2001. $15

The Cartoon Gospel (of Luke), ISBN 978-0-9702244-1-5, December, 1990.
$15

Note: Prices may change without notice. See www.the-cartoonist.com
for current prices, updates and new releases!

Quick Order Form

Online orders: order directly from the web at www.the-cartoonist.com

E-Mail orders: send this completed order form (as a PDF or .jpg file) to:
orders@the-cartoonist.com

Mail Order: send to Diesslin Press, 1366 Town Hall Rd., Dayton, OH 45432

Please send the following books, CDs or e-books. I understand that I may return any of them within 30 days for a full refund - for any reason, no questions asked.

_____
_____
_____

Please send more FREE information on:

___ Books   ___ Speaking   ___ Custom Cartooning

Name: _____

Address: _____

City: _____ State: ____ Zip:_____

Telephone: _____ Email:_____

Autograph: ___ (Y/N) to (optional): _____

Shipping and Handling:
Regular mail in the U.S.: $2.50 (first class and media mail).
By air:
U.S.: $4.00 for first book and $1.00 for each additional product.
International: $5.00 for the first book, $2.00 for each additional product.

Payment: Check enclosed for $_____ to Diesslin Press

Note: For credit/debit card orders, please order online at www.the-cartoonist.com